our
generation.

This is Coco's story.

COCO ™

WRITING WITH CHOCOLATE

BY

LAURA LEIGH MOTTE

ILLUSTRATED BY GÉRALDINE CHARETTE

An Our Generation® *book*

MAISON BATTAT INC. *Publisher*

To all those children with challenges to overcome. Courage! You can do it! And to everyone who loves chocolate.

Read all the adventures in the
Our Generation® Book Series

Read more about **Our Generation®** books and dolls online:
ourgeneration.com

CONTENTS

EXTRA! EXTRA! READ ALL ABOUT IT!
*Big words, wacky words, powerful words, funny words...
what do they all mean? They are marked with this symbol *.
Look them up in the Glossary at the end of this book.*

Chapter One

THE CASE OF THE FLYING CHOCOLATE FONDUE

All I know is this: One second, I was carrying a bowl of melted chocolate down the school hallway. The next second, the bowl of chocolate was all over Cambi Laflamme's butterfly sweater.

Picture-perfect, princess-perfect Cambi Laflamme stood there, frozen, looking down at her sweater. The butterfly was smeared with chocolate.

Drip. Drip. Drip.

That was the sound of the chocolate dripping off Cambi's sweater and falling onto the floor. The chocolate formed a puddle around her feet.

I watched, in a daze*, as the puddle slowly

grew larger, finally stopping at a pair of yellow sneakers.

I looked up. The yellow sneakers belonged to Mrs. Hayward. She is the Vice Principal. She was wearing jogging pants and a jacket. It was strange. Normally, Mrs. Hayward wears a skirt and a blouse buttoned right up to the top. But today wasn't a normal day. It was a Saturday. The day of Amesville Elementary School's famous Valentine's Day Craft and Bake Sale.

"What on Earth happened here?" she asked Cambi, as she stepped back from the chocolate puddle.

Cambi couldn't speak. She was a chocolate statue.

"I think I spilled chocolate on Cambi," I mumbled.

Mrs. Hayward looked at me, eyebrows raised.

"Cordelia, were you running in the hallway again?"

I bit my lip. It's true. I have a reputation

for breaking speed limits. Especially in the school hallways. It mostly happens when I'm doing my duties as class messenger for the third grade. I'm superfast. Hermes, the Greek god we studied in our mythology chapter, with his winged feet, can't compete with me and my superfast sneakers, or loafers, or sandals—actually, I bet I could beat him in a pair of flip-flops. That's how fast my feet can go. Nothing can stop me.

Nothing except Mrs. Hayward.

When she catches someone running in the hallway, she gives them a speeding ticket. I already had two speeding tickets. Would this be number three? I heard that students with three speeding tickets get kicked out of school.

But was I really speeding? I wasn't so sure. And, if I wasn't speeding, how did all that melted chocolate end up on Cambi's sweater?

Then it hit me. I had many reasons not to like her.

Oh dear... Would I have... Could I have...

Done it on purpose?

To find out the answer, I'll have to go back to the beginning, to when it all started.

Chapter Two

THE NEED FOR SPEED

First, let me just say that normally, I am the one with the chocolate on my face. Or on my nose. Sometimes it's on my shoes. And yes, plenty of times I've had chocolate on my sweater.

I love chocolate more than anything. More than pink scooters, pickle-flavored potato chips, and sparkly slime. Chocolate is the best thing in the world. I like it on my toast, in my cookies, folded inside my banana muffins, and sprinkled on my breakfast cereal. I even like it on my chicken (it's a spicy sauce called *mole* and it's delicious).

Chocolate isn't just my favorite food, it's my favorite color. You may think that's weird, but chocolate goes with everything.

Pink. Orange. Turquoise.

That's why my parents nicknamed me "Coco." Not only is it easier to say than Cordelia Columbia, which is my real name, it's also the main ingredient in chocolate. Well, if you add an "a," which makes it cocoa.

Dad sometimes calls me "Coco Loco*" because I'm crazy about chocolate, and I'm full of energy. I like to jump and skip and run around. I love races too. Because I'm so fast.

With three older brothers, I have no choice. My parents try to keep things fair. It's not easy. I've learned the hard way that if you go slow, you lose out. Like the time my mom made one of her special homemade chocolate cakes. I was five years old and still learning to hold my fork the right way. While I took my time, my brothers had seconds and thirds. Before I knew it, all the cake was gone. I cried so much my eyes hurt.

Since then, I am always first. I'm first in the bathroom in the morning, first to brush my teeth, first to get dressed, and first to the breakfast table. A house full of hungry older brothers is a jungle. It's Survival of the Fastest.

On school days, I set my alarm clock extra early. I lay out my clothes the night before and test out my speedy slide. My speedy slide is a slide my dad attached to my bed. It's faster and more fun than climbing down the steps. Kind of like when a fireman hears "Fire!"—only I hear "Breakfast!"

I've even been trying a neat new trick: putting my shoes at the bottom of the slide, then sliding my feet right into them as I reach the floor. Once I get this part right, there'll be no stopping me!

But this morning, there was a problem. Shaya, my oldest brother, was up early too. When I opened my bedroom door, he was opening his. We looked at each other, eyes narrowing. The race was on.

Luckily my bedroom is closer to the staircase. I skipped down the stairs, taking two

at a time, then skidded into the kitchen. I ran straight for the cupboards. Shaya came in a split second later. But it was too late.

"Got it!" I said, snatching a box of Choco Yum Yums cereal. I shook the box. There was only a little bit left.

"It's all yours, Coco Loco," Shaya sighed. He grabbed a packet of hot cereal. Mom says it's healthy because it has no added sugar. All I know is that it has no added chocolate. What's the point?

After a while, Mika and Roman charged into the kitchen. They're my twin brothers, identical in every way. They both wear glasses with thick lenses and black rims. They look gentle and sweet. But be careful. They're rascals.

"Last one to the stop sign is a dirty rotten egg!" Mika shouted.

I jumped out of my seat, ready to race. Since we all go to Amesville Elementary School,

Mika and Roman and I walk to school together. Often, we race.

As I reached for my coat, Mika grinned. "Psych," he said, taking my seat at the table and finishing the last of my Choco Yum Yums. He and Roman high-fived.

I sighed. *Brothers!*

❧ ❧

At school, when I got to class, my best friend, Mei, was already at her desk. I've known her since kindergarten—which is a very long time to know someone.

I was about to sit at my desk next to her, then stopped myself. *Ugh! I keep forgetting.*

After the holiday break, our teacher, Miss Pennyfield, had separated us. She said we talked too much. She moved Cambi Laflamme to the front of the classroom next to Mei. Then she moved me to the back of the classroom, by the fish tank. That's where Scaly and Slimy live.

They're the classroom goldfish.

The desk beside me is empty. A girl named Manuela used to sit there. I called her "Absent" because she was never here. For the first month of school, she had a broken leg. Then she had the flu. For Christmas, she went to visit her grandparents in Portugal. Her family must have liked it there because Miss Pennyfield said they weren't coming back.

"Mei!" Cambi squealed as she came over to her seat, which used to be my seat. "Look what I got." She unzipped her butterfly pencil case and pulled out a set of pens.

"They're for calligraphy*."

Cambi scribbled a few letters on a piece of paper and showed Mei.

"If you draw over it with this, it changes color!" Cambi demonstrated in a page of her notebook. "Isn't that neat?"

"Very!" Mei gushed.

I frowned as I watched the two of them chatting.

"I have a set of glitter gel pens at home," said Mei. "Imagine using both of them at the same time?"

"We could make letters that change color *and* sparkle!" said Cambi.

Since they began sitting together, I noticed the two of them becoming friends. Cambi really likes butterflies. She has a butterfly sweater, a butterfly purse, and butterfly stickers that she puts on all her binders. Today, I noticed Mei had a butterfly sticker on her binder too. I wondered when that happened.

Cambi had even asked Mei to her butterfly-themed birthday party. Scaly and Slimy never asked me to any of their birthday parties.

Swoosh! A piece of paper landed on my desk. It was my last spelling test. I snatched it up eagerly. I couldn't wait to see my grade. I had known almost all the words and I was the very first to finish. (I feel I should get bonus marks for that.)

Then I saw the red circles and question

marks all over the test paper. And the grade. I gasped.

Four out of ten!?

How was that possible? I knew all the words. Like the first one, *principal*. That one was easy. You just have to remember this: *A principal is your pal.* Because the word principal always ends with a *p, a,* and *l.*

But even that one was marked with a big red X.

I looked closer. Beside the grade, Miss Pennyfield had written a note in red:

IMPOSSIBLE TO READ!
CORDELIA, YOU MUST
IMPROVE YOUR HANDWRITING!

I cleared my throat and raised my hand.

"Yes, Cordelia?" Miss Pennyfield said.

"I think there's something wrong with my test."

Miss Pennyfield walked over to my desk.

I lifted my paper and pointed to the first word. "Principal is right. See?"

"Yes, Cordelia. I'm sure that was your intention. But when I am marking your test, I don't know what you *meant* to write, I only see the letters on the page. I have to ask myself, is the last letter an *e*, or an *l*? If I can't tell, I must mark it wrong. It was the same with 'puddle' and 'scout.' It's been a problem on your other class work too."

"I don't understand," I said.

"I know," Miss Pennyfield said. "Show this test to your parents. You can tell them someone from the school will be calling to talk to them about it."

"Really?"

"Yes. I think it's high time* we fixed the problem of me not being able to read your mind."

Miss Pennyfield gave me a smile and continued handing back the tests.

I swallowed hard. In all my three and

a half years of elementary school, no teacher had ever, *ever* called my parents to discuss something.

This was serious.

Chapter Three

THE CALLIGRAPHY CLUB

I love the cafeteria. In the cafeteria, we can sit wherever we want. Today, I was sitting with Mei in our usual spot by the window, overlooking the playing field. A few sixth-grade boys were playing football. Snowflakes swirled and danced around the boys like they wanted to play too.

All around us, chairs scraped the floor as other students took their seats. Lunch boxes were unzipped. Sandwiches unwrapped. Juice boxes poked with straws.

"Mei, can I get your opinion on something?" I had to raise my voice over all the noise. "Mrs. Pennyfield says my handwriting is impossible to read."

I handed Mei my spelling test. As she

unfolded the paper and looked it over, I tore off the lid of my chocolate pudding cup. (I always eat my chocolate pudding first.)

"What do you think?" I asked, licking the lid.

"Well..." Mei paused. "It is a little hard to read."

I stopped licking. That wasn't the answer I was expecting.

"Oh, who cares about handwriting?" I said, snatching the paper back, and then stuffing it in my pocket. "Nobody needs to write anymore. With a computer, you can speak, and the computer will type out your words for you! You don't even need to spell! Writing is for dinosaurs."

"That's one way of looking at it," Mei replied quietly.

As I dipped an apple slice in my chocolate pudding cup, Cambi walked up to our table.

"Hi, Mei. Hi, Cordelia," she said, twirling a strand of red hair around her finger. The

rhinestones* in her butterfly barrettes sparkled in the sunlight.

"It's Coco," I corrected her. "Only teachers call me Cordelia."

She nodded, then pointed to my face. "You have chocolate on your nose."

"Oops." I quickly wiped my nose with the back of my hand.

Then she turned to Mei.

"Mei, would you like to come to my house after school? We can use my new calligraphy pens to make title pages for our Greek mythology booklets."

Mei's eyes lit up*.

"That sounds like fun!"

"We'll have our very own calligraphy club!" Cambi squealed, clasping her hands together like this was the most exciting thing to happen at Amesville Elementary School.

"I've always wanted to be in a club," Mei said.

I crossed my arms tightly. I had hoped

to invite Mei to *my* house after school—but Cambi Laflamme and her fancy new pens beat me to it.

See what I mean about Survival of the Fastest? When you want something, you have to be quick. Go too slow, you lose out.

Chapter Four

TRUFFLES

"Is this new?" my mother asked. "I love the layers of old paint." She ran her fingers down the back of a chair that looked like it had been left out in the rain for a year. The paint was peeling off and there were at least three different colors underneath.

"Me too," Aunt Joonie replied. "I used a clear varnish over it to preserve the look. It's so dreamy."

We were in my Aunt Joonie's shop. It's called "Joonie's Treasures" and it's full of old stuff. Old dressers, old lamps, even old blankets. She calls them "antiques." I call them "icky." I prefer new things. New socks, new T-shirts, new sneakers that squeak on the floor until you break them in. I like things that come in cardboard boxes, wrapped in layers of plastic with little bubbles in them that make popping noises when I jump on them.

As Aunt Joonie and Mom chatted about how great old stuff is, I fiddled with the keys on an old cash register. It was pink with silver keys. When I pressed a big button, the drawer popped out with a loud ding.

"A million dollars, please!" I said, putting out my hand to my mother, pretending I was the store owner. "That chair is one-of-a-kind. They don't make them that ugly anymore."

Aunt Joonie laughed. "Sorry, but I can't let it go for any less than *two* million," she said. "Chairs this ugly don't grow on trees."

I giggled. Aunt Joonie and I get along well, even though she is not really my aunt. She is my mom's best friend from school. Just like me and Mei, they've known each other since kindergarten. I guess you can call them "BFFs."

Mom likes to visit Aunt Joonie's shop whenever she has free time on a Saturday. I go with her too, not because I like junk, but because I like chocolate.

"Can we go now?" I asked. "I'm hungry."

Aunt Joonie put a "Be Back Soon" sign in the window and we headed out to Main Street.

Though Amesville is a small town, the downtown gets busy on the weekends. Even tourists from the big city come to check it out. All the downtown buildings are old, but they look new because they're painted in pretty colors. Joonie's Treasures is bright yellow.

A block away from Aunt Joonie's store is *La Chocolaterie*. It's a chocolate boutique* that sells homemade chocolates and all kinds of other yummy stuff with chocolate in it. The outside is painted light blue.

Today, the glass windows were frosted over but you could still see the pyramids of chocolate truffles* surrounded by dangling gold, green, and shimmering ruby* streamers.

The next display would be for Valentine's Day. There was a ladder in the window. On the floor beside it, the angels and stars were already packed inside a cardboard box.

"Brrrr," Mom said, buttoning up her coat and putting on the cap I had given her for Christmas. The cold made me crave one thing and one thing only.

❦ ❦

"Who ordered the hot chocolate with whipped cream and caramel swirl and sprinkles on top?" the server asked.

I raised my hand.

The server placed the steaming mug in front of me. I warmed my hands on the sides. We were lucky to get a spot in a cozy booth with a curved, blue velvet seat.

Behind the counter, Chloe, the owner, was stirring a pot of her famous melted caramel. She sells it in mason jars wrapped in pretty cloth on a shelf next to the packets of hot chocolate. On the counter, a batch of brownies was cooling. The whole room smelled like butter, sugar, and

cocoa. It was heavenly.

When she saw me, Chloe waved. "Hi, Coco." We go there often so she knows us by name.

"Where's Mei?" she asked. Mei usually joins us on our Saturday outings to downtown Amesville.

"Busy," I said, sipping my hot chocolate. It was hot and burned my tongue. "She has a new friend," I added, softly, so only Mom and Aunt Joonie could hear. "They started a calligraphy club."

As I said it, a tear slowly rolled down my cheek and dropped into my hot chocolate.

"Oh dear," Mom said, shifting closer to me on the seat. "That happens sometimes. Friends can drift apart. But they can also come back together."

"Can't you do calligraphy *with* them?" Aunt Joonie asked. "It sounds like fun."

"No," I replied. My faced turned a little red.

"Why not?" Mom asked.

"They didn't ask me."

I turned away and looked across the room. I noticed the writing on the menu board in white chalk:

Try Our Newest Truffles!
Chocolate Cherry
Chipotle Chili
Orange Jasmine

Normally, I'd be thinking of how yummy they all sounded. But today, the chalk letters on the board, with their fancy curls, made me think of something else: the spelling test crumpled up in my pocket and the words Miss Pennyfield had written in red pen.

I decided it was time to tell Mom the truth. I couldn't hold it inside anymore. At least here my brothers weren't around to make fun of me.

I took the test out of my pocket and

handed it to my mom.

"Maybe this is why Mei didn't ask me."

"Oh," she said, sitting up straight on the sofa. She reached inside her purse and pulled out her reading glasses.

I watched nervously as her eyes scanned the test. Left. Right. Left. Right. Finally, she spoke.

"Your teacher seems to have a very strong opinion about your handwriting."

"Yes," I replied. "Miss Pennyfield says someone from the school will be calling you about it. Do you think my writing is so terrible?"

"Well, I have to admit, Coco, that I *have* noticed that your handwriting can be a bit..." She paused for a moment before finding the right word. "*Wild*. But I never worried because you're so bright and perfect in every other way."

My frown curled up into a half smile. "Thanks, Mom."

"But maybe your teacher is right. Maybe it's time we gave this issue some attention."

"Mr. Vanhorne never had a problem with my writing," I argued.

"That was last year. You're halfway through third grade now."

I let out a soft sigh. I wanted to cry, but I stopped myself. Mom put an arm around me. "Honey, don't you want to improve your handwriting? Not just for school, but for *you?*"

I looked at the menu board again, and the pretty letters Chloe drew so effortlessly with her chalk. Then, I thought about Mei and how, at this very moment, she and Cambi were using their fancy pens to make title pages for their Greek Mythology Booklets.

"Maybe," I admitted softly. "Maybe I do."

"So, let's take care of it." Mom clapped her hands together. "You know what? I'm not going to wait for the school to call me. I'm going to call your teacher Monday morning and find out more about this plan to help you."

I nodded.

I was relieved to have finally shown my mother the test. But I was also nervous.

What kind of plan did they have in mind?

Chapter Five

THE I CAN'T ROOM

A few days later, Miss Delphine showed up in my classroom.

"Cordelia Columbia?" she said, reading my name from a piece of paper in her hand, then looking around the room.

All eyes turned to me.

Miss Delphine is the school's occupational therapist*.

Every week, sometimes twice a week, Miss Delphine takes children with learning problems to a special room called the "I CAN" room where she helps them improve. Last year, Noah Coates went there. He used to have trouble using scissors. This year, his paper snowflake was the prettiest one in the classroom window. When we took them down, Miss Pennyfield asked if she could keep his snowflake for next Christmas. From the way Noah nodded and grinned, I could tell he was proud of himself.

But some students have another name for the I CAN room. They call it the "I CAN'T" room. They're not supposed to, but they do. Today, it was me who was going to the I CAN'T room.

I wanted to run, or hide under my desk, or jump into the fish tank with Scaly and Slimy. But I knew it was useless. I had to do this.

I stood up and made my way over to the doorway where Miss Delphine was standing. It was the longest walk of my entire life.

The I CAN room is on the other side of the school, near the gym. Since I'm the class messenger, I know all the rooms in the school. I know the Staff Room, the Library (which has a secret entrance that the librarian showed me one day), the Vice Principal's Office, the Principal's Office, the Nurse's Office, and all the classrooms from kindergarten to grade six.

But I'd never been inside the I CAN room.

When Miss Delphine took me inside, I was amazed. It looked like a playroom. There were boxes of beads and string on a table, yarn and knitting needles in baskets. There were toys, blocks, tons of colored pencils and markers, big pads of paper on easels, a gym mat, and even a swing! There was also a little kitchen area with a microwave oven, plastic bowls, and utensils.

"What does all this have to do with handwriting?" I asked her.

"You'll see," she said with a mysterious smile.

The first thing she did was give me a bunch of tests. She made me put beads on a string, color inside some lines, and copy a text. I did them all superfast.

Miss Delphine must have been impressed because she took notes after each exercise.

"You did well, Cordelia."

I stood up from my chair. "I knew it!" I was sure Miss Pennyfield was wrong.

Then Miss Delphine added, "With a little work, we can definitely improve your handwriting."

I frowned. *I have to come back?*

As I thought about that on the way back to my classroom, I saw Cambi in the hallway. I looked at the wall clock. There were still seven minutes until recess. What was she doing out of class? That's when I noticed she was carrying a message in her hand. She must have seen me looking at it, because she held the paper up in the air.

"It's a message for the nurse," she chirped, swinging her red hair back. "Miss Pennyfield made me class messenger while you're in the I CAN room on Tuesdays and Thursdays. I hope I can be as fast as you are!"

As she skipped down the hallway, I shook my head. I couldn't believe it.

Not only was Cambi Laflamme a Friend Stealer, she was a Job Stealer too.

Chapter Six

FLORENCE

The following Thursday, when I went back to the I CAN room, there was another girl in the room.

I'd seen her around the school before. With her blonde, curly hair she is hard to miss. Her name is Florence. She's in Mrs. Huntsberger's classroom and has something called autism*. I knew this word because Shaya's best friend, Elliot, has a little brother who is in the same class. He has autism too.

When she saw me, she held up her hand, like a police officer stopping traffic. "Be careful, the table is sticky."

Florence used the edge of a ruler to scrape a piece of leftover modeling clay that had stuck to the worktable. It seemed important to her, and she was working hard.

"There. All gone," she said, putting her ruler away in her pencil case. "Now I'm going to wipe it clean so there's no stickiness left." She pulled out a plastic case from her backpack. In the case was a stack of small, wet cloths.

"I always have some of these handy, just in case," she said. "I don't like being sticky."

Florence finished cleaning the table with the cloth and then pulled out a chair. "There, you can take a seat now. There's no stickiness left."

I thought it was very nice of her. But I was still confused. What was she doing in my session with Miss Delphine?

That's when Miss Delphine came into the room.

"Ah, I see you two have met. Good." She was carrying a stack of binders and other supplies.

"Do you like bugs?" Florence asked me.

"They're OK," I said. "Except when

they're under my pillow. My twin brothers are always putting fake plastic spiders under my pillow or in my shoes. One time they put a plastic spider in my lunch box."

"What kind of spider was it?" Florence asked. "There are many species."

"The creepy kind?" I said with a grin.

Florence frowned. "That's not a species."

"Oh," I said. "That's not what I—"

"The Araneomorphae is the biggest group," Florence went on. "They are divided into two main subgroups: the Haplogynae and the Entelegynae…"

As she carried on about spiders, I looked at Miss Delphine. Huh?

"I think you need to learn the Golden Rule of Florence," she said.

"Rule?"

"I have a problem with jokes," explained Florence. "I don't always understand them."

"That's why you have to give her a little 'wink wink,'" Miss Delphine added. "You can also say 'Ha ha. Joke.' It's a little trick that helps her understand that what you are saying is not to be taken literally*."

"OK." That rule seemed simple enough to follow.

"Are you ready for your first exercise?" Miss Delphine said, pulling out a timer. "You have twenty seconds to write a word of your choice. It should be at least eight letters. And don't tell me the word." Miss Delphine handed us each a piece of paper and a pencil. "Just hold it in your mind and be ready when I tell you to write it down."

As I was thinking, I was feeling hungry. Not hungry for food. Hungry for chocolate. Then I remembered there was still a truffle left from *La Chocolaterie*. It was in a little pink box tucked in the back of the fridge so my brothers wouldn't see it. Suddenly, the word came to me.

I quickly wrote it down. Then I looked over at Florence. She was furiously erasing and rewriting.

"Time's up," said Miss Delphine. She took both our sheets and sat down with us to look at them. We looked at Florence's first.

"L-a...?" I said.

"It's supposed to be *ladybugs*," said Florence. "They're my favorite bug. But I didn't finish it in time."

When I looked again at the word, I could see the faint traces of the letter *d*.

"Why did you erase the *d*?" Miss Delphine asked.

"The bump wasn't round enough," explained Florence.

"But we know it's a *d*. Even erased, it looks like a *d*. Right, Cordelia?"

I nodded.

"That's the first goal in writing," said Miss Delphine. "Making sure each letter is readable. Not pretty, or perfect, just readable. Sometimes you need to give up the idea of being perfect, and just get the job done. When you don't finish the word, the word can't make sense to us. It's not *ladybugs*, it's *la*."

"Do re mi fa so la…!" I sang. Then I looked at Florence with a wink. "Joke."

Florence smiled.

"OK guys. My turn." I turned my page around to face them.

Florence looked at the word. She squinted hard, turned her head sideways…

"Inoculatt?"

"Seriously?!" I sighed. "Come on." I looked over at Miss Delphine for help.

"I'm stumped too," she said.

"It's chocolate!" I said, giving up.

"That's a *c*?" asked Florence. "It looks more like an *i*."

"That's because Cordelia is writing too fast," Miss Delphine explained. "She's not paying attention to the form of each letter. She's rushing to the finish line."

But instead of being upset with me, Miss Delphine smiled. "Isn't it fascinating?"

I was confused.

"How is my bad handwriting fascinating?" I asked.

"Because you both have the opposite issues. Cordelia, you're like a high-speed train. You get your word done, but you don't take enough time to consider the size and proportion of each letter. You can't read it."

She turned to Florence.

"For you, Florence, it's all about being perfect. You take so much time making each letter so perfect that you can't make it over the finish line."

"That's true," said Florence. Her chin dropped and she stared at the ground sadly.

"Don't be sad," Miss Delphine said with a smile. "This is a good thing. That's why I put you girls together. I think you can learn from one another."

Florence and I looked at each other and shrugged.

This wasn't going to be easy.

Chapter Seven

A NEW KIND OF PEN

"Who ate my truffle!?" I shouted at no one in particular. I was standing in the kitchen, holding an empty pink box.

Roman walked into the kitchen. He saw me holding the truffle box and grinned.

"It was very tasty," he said, laughing and running back upstairs.

I didn't bother running after him.

I looked around the kitchen. There was one banana in the fruit bowl, but it didn't seem too exciting.

I rifled* through the cupboards and drawers, banging them open and closed.

"What are you looking for?" Shaya asked as he came into the kitchen.

"Chocolate," I replied.

"Coco Loco, on the hunt," Shaya grinned.

"Always." Sometimes my brother Shaya isn't so bad.

From the drawer with baking sheets* and measuring cups, I pulled out a bar of baking chocolate.

I waved the bar at Shaya. "Found some!"

"Isn't that stuff bitter*?" Shaya asked.

Shaya was right. Baking chocolate is different from a regular chocolate bar. It's not as sweet. But I knew how to fix the problem.

"That's why we're going to turn it into fondue!" I'd seen Mom do it plenty of times. It wasn't that hard.

Shaya helped me melt the chocolate in the microwave. I added sugar and whisked the melted chocolate as fast as I could. A few splatters of chocolate flew onto the countertop. One of them landed on my blouse. I wiped it off with my finger and tasted it. Just right!

Shaya sliced up the banana and we used forks to dip the slices into the fondue. It was scrumptious*. As we feasted, I took out the worksheets Miss Delphine had given me.

"Those are weird," said Shaya.

"I know, right?"

On each page, there were a series of loops that looked like soft round hilltops. Another set of lines looked like jagged mountains. I had to trace over them. Miss Delphine wanted three pages of each for the next session.

I looked at the clock. Almost five. I didn't have much time. Roman may have gotten my truffle, but he wasn't going to win The Battle for Dad's Tablet.

✿ ✿

It was our next session in the I CAN room and Florence was showing Miss Delphine her completed worksheets.

"They're very well done," Miss Delphine said.

I looked over their shoulders at Florence's

worksheet. Her traces of jagged mountains and loops were perfect.

"But you only did one sheet," Miss Delphine said.

Florence shrugged. "My pointy mountains aren't as pointy as they could be. I had to redo them a few times. They're still not perfect."

I looked at her sheet more closely. Her pointy mountains looked perfectly pointy to me.

"Coco, do you have your sheets?" Miss Delphine asked.

I pulled out my sheets.

"You did them all, which is great," Miss Delphine said, scanning over each line with her finger. Florence looked impressed too.

"But your tracings are a little loose. See here?" She held up a page. "You've crossed over the line almost every time. And many of your loops are pointy instead of round. She put the sheets down and looked at me.

"I feel these may have been a little rushed.

Am I right?"

Her green eyes seemed to peer right through me.

"I always do my homework fast," I said. "If I beat my brothers, I get first dibs on Dad's tablet. He has all the good games."

"Ah ha!" said Miss Delphine. "Well, Cordelia, sometimes in life, and especially in writing, we can't rush. We may not get Dad's tablet, but we get the reward of doing a job well. It's OK to slow down, Coco. In school, there's never a prize for finishing first, is there?"

"No," I replied. I remembered thinking the same thing about my spelling test and wondering why there were no bonus marks for finishing first. Now I knew the answer.

"It's about quality, not speed," Miss Delphine said, handing me back my exercises.

"What's this?" she asked, pointing to a smear on my worksheet.

"Chocolate," I said.

"How did the chocolate get on the paper?

Did you use a chocolate pen?"

Florence looked shocked. "I thought we were supposed to use colored markers?"

"Joke," Miss Delphine said, looking at Florence. "There are no chocolate pens."

"Oh," Florence nodded.

"There *should* be," I blurted out. "Then we could eat our mistakes."

I looked at Florence and winked.

This time, Florence giggled. "That's so funny!" Her big smile showed off two dimples, one on each side of her rosy cheeks. I had never noticed them before.

"Actually," Miss Delphine said, biting her lip thoughtfully. "Maybe it's not a joke."

With a mysterious look, she pushed the worksheets aside and stood up. "Follow me," she said, leading us into the kitchen area of the I CAN room. From a drawer, she took out some baking chocolate and trays. I was amazed she had so many cooking ingredients.

Miss Delphine told us she uses baking

projects, like making cakes and cookies, to help kids build up hand strength, work their fine motor skills*, loosen up their wrists, and follow sequences*.

She showed us how to make piping bags* out of parchment paper*. We melted chocolate chips in the microwave, then let them cool a few minutes before pouring them into the piping bags.

"What are we making?" I asked.

"Pens," she said. "But instead of being filled with ink, they're filled with chocolate."

Laying out more parchment paper on the table, Miss Delphine asked us to write our names in chocolate, using the piping bags. I started writing right away.

"Slow down, Cordelia," said Miss Delphine. "It's not a race. Would you prefer chocolate in your tummy? Or on the floor or smeared all over your worksheet?"

I thought about this. "Chocolate in my tummy."

"So, take your time," she said.

As I worked on the chocolate letters, I remembered what Miss Delphine had told us about writing, like how to keep the right proportions and shapes. My heads* had to reach up. My tails* needed to stretch down low.

Suddenly, it wasn't a race. It was just fun.

When I wrote my first *o* it looked more like an *a*. I erased it with a small spatula and licked it clean.

"Yummy mistake," I said.

Florence, who was now familiar with the joke, grinned.

"I'm going to make a mistake too, just so I can eat it," said Florence.

"Go for it!" said Miss Delphine. "Make a mistake. It's OK!"

Miss Delphine looked at me, her eyes wide with surprise. I guessed this was something special for Florence.

"Coco, I think you are onto something

with this chocolate writing." She gave me a wink.

I smiled. Miss Delphine had a way of making me feel special, even if I wasn't perfect.

As Florence and I wrote our names in chocolate, the I CAN room felt like a magical place where anything was possible. And where mistakes were as delicious as a chocolate truffle.

Chapter Eight

CHOCOLATE HOMEWORK

After school, I couldn't wait to do more chocolate "homework."

Miss Delphine had given me a list of words that she had chosen just for me. They all had letters with heads or tails on them. Like a cat. Miss Delphine gave me this as an example:

Mom and I melted chocolate chips in the microwave. I showed her my new technique*, using the piping bag as my "chocolate pen."

My first word was *happy*.

Mika and Roman gathered round to watch as I made my chocolate letters. They kept trying to dip their fingers into my bowl of melted chocolate.

"Stop that!" I shouted. "It's not a snack. It's homework!" I waved my wooden spoon at them.

"Chocolate homework," said Roman. "Who ever heard of that?"

"I invented it," I said proudly. "Miss Delphine said I was her *inspiration*."

"It's genius, darling," Mom said, grabbing the bowl of chocolate away from Mika's reach as he was about to plunge another finger in the bowl. "Maybe it's time you boys did your own homework."

"Fine," Mika said, sneaking one last fingerful.

"Last one upstairs is a dirty rotten egg!" Roman cried, and they both stampeded* out of the room.

After my chocolate words were all written and cooled, I noticed a problem. When I tried to pick them up, they broke easily. They were too thin. For my next chocolate letter, I wanted something more solid, something that I could hold in my hand or put in a box. Like a truffle.

That's when I got an idea. Using a stencil from my pencil case, I traced the capital* letters onto the parchment paper. I spelled C O C O. Then I filled in the letters with chocolate. I layered it on thick. They looked really solid.

Then I had another idea.

"Let's decorate them!"

At *La Chocolaterie*, they always mix interesting flavors into their chocolates. I dug out some candy sprinkles from the baking drawer. I found a leftover Christmas candy cane in the bottom of the drawer, so I crushed that up too. Then I sprinkled the candy on the chocolate letters.

"Look Mom! Aren't they pretty?"

"Pretty enough to sell at *La Chocolaterie*," Mom said, admiring my work.

I held back from eating them. I wanted to show Florence and Miss Delphine.

I looked in the living room. Mika and Roman had taken Dad's tablet and were sitting on the sofa playing "Chase the Squirrel." They'd finished their homework a long time ago. I'd missed my chance. But I didn't care. I remembered what Miss Delphine had said. Everything isn't a race.

∾ ∽

"As you already know," said Miss Pennyfield to the class, with a big smile, "Amesville Elementary School's famous Valentine's Day Craft and Bake Sale is happening in a few weeks. There are still a few booths left. If anyone wants to participate, now's the time!"

Last year, I went to the sale with my mom. She bought me a homemade bracelet. Two fifth-grade girls had made it using heart-shaped beads. Their booth was called "Just Bead It."

I remembered thinking how fun it would be to have my very own booth. But I had no idea what I'd do. Now I did! When the bell rang, I leapt out of my seat to catch up with Mei. She was already out in the hallway.

"Mei!" I called.

I ran down the hall at top speed, flying past a row of lockers and spinning around the janitor, who was crossing the hall with his cleaning cart.

"Stop right there, Cordelia!"

Chapter Nine

COCOA BY COCO

It was the Vice Principal. My sneakers squeaked to a halt.

"You know the rules, Cordelia. No running in the halls."

"Sorry Mrs. Hayward," I gasped, out of breath.

Mrs. Hayward pulled a pad of paper from a pocket inside her suit jacket.

"I'm afraid I'm going to have to give you another ticket," she said, clicking her pen with her thumb and scribbling on the pad.

I was worried. *One more and it'll be three.* I didn't know what happened when you got three speeding tickets. But I was too afraid to ask.

After the ticket was written and I folded it

into my binder, I was finally free.

Down the hall, I saw Cambi and Mei talking.

"A calligraphy booth is a great idea," I heard Cambi say.

"Oh no," I moaned. She and Mei were obviously going to have a booth together. Once again, Cambi had beaten me to the finish line and all because of Mrs. Hayward and her silly speeding tickets. (This Vice Principal was definitely not my "pal.")

"We can make Valentine's Day cards," Cambi said. "It's perfect."

Mei nodded. "Yes! We can write messages on them about love and friendship and stuff like that. We can use our special pens. My dad has lots of pretty paper at his office. I'm sure he'll give us some."

They didn't know I was behind them because then I heard Mei say this:

"Should we ask Coco?"

"You told me she doesn't like calligraphy,"

Cambi said. "She said handwriting is for dinosaurs, which wasn't very nice."

I cringed. I'd totally forgotten about that.

I debated walking over to them and explaining. I wanted to tell them that the only reason I said that was because I was upset about my own writing.

But I stopped myself. My handwriting was still a work in progress, and I had a long way to go. Besides, I had another idea for the booth. A better idea. Chocolate.

That's when I saw Florence. She was cleaning her locker with one of her wet wipes.

"Stupid gum," she said. "Don't people know to put it in the garbage?"

Her locker was decorated with ladybug stickers. On the top shelf of her locker there was a book. The title was big enough for me to read: "The History of Chocolate." I smiled. Miss Delphine's session in the I CAN room had obviously inspired her too.

At that moment, I knew who my partner

should be.

"Hey Florence," I said. "Do you want to do a chocolate booth for the Valentine's Day Craft and Bake Sale?"

Florence tossed her wet wipe into her locker and jumped into the air.

"Yes! What a great idea, Coco."

"I thought we could do the same kind of chocolate homework we were doing in the I CAN room, but with a Valentine's Day twist. We can make chocolate hearts and even some of those letter molds I showed you the other day. People can spell mom or friend or love or—"

"Ladybug!" said Florence.

Suddenly, she frowned. She reached into her locker and pulled out her calendar. She flipped through it quickly, stopped at a page, and then groaned, "Oh no."

"What is it?" I asked.

"I have to go to the Insectarium that Saturday. It's a special exhibit of extra rare

bugs. There's even a luna moth!"

"Can't you change the date?" I asked.

"That's impossible!" she said, her eyes wide. "Once something is written down in my calendar, I can't change it."

"Oh," I said. I would have been angry, but I knew from the I CAN room that Florence hates changing schedules as much as she hates stickiness. Once we wanted to change our I CAN session to Wednesday instead of Tuesday, and she got really upset.

Down the hallway, Mei and Cambi were still talking about their Valentine's Day Card booth.

"We can write messages on T-shirts," said Mei. "I saw fabric markers at the craft store that would totally work."

"I've always wanted to try that," said Cambi. They walked down the hallway and their voices trailed off.

I wondered if I should run after them, but I didn't.

I was on my own.

☙ ❧

I stood by the ice-covered bike racks, waiting for my brothers to join me for our walk home. My feet were still, but my mind was racing.

I really wanted to do a chocolate booth but doing it on my own seemed impossible.

I thought about asking my mom and Aunt Joonie. Having Mom and Aunt Joonie around would be a big help, for sure. But I also wanted someone my age. I wanted, well, *a friend*.

I was so distracted, thinking and worrying about my chocolate booth, that I dropped my glove on the ground. When I leaned down to pick it up, another hand beat me to it. It was Florence. She was bundled up for the cold in a caramel-colored coat, brown hat, and boots. She looked as yummy as a salted caramel truffle.

"My dad and I have a solution," she said, handing me my glove. In the parking area behind us, her father was waiting in his car. He gave me a friendly wave.

"I know I can't be at the sale, but I can still help you make the chocolates. My dad and I looked at my calendar together and I'm free every Monday, Wednesday, and Friday after school for the next two weeks. But I can't possibly do Tuesday or Thursday. What do you think?"

"Of course!" I said. I instantly felt better. Florence had come to my rescue.

Then I had another idea.

"Maybe we can donate the money we make to the I CAN room," I suggested. "I remember last year, some of the booths raised money for the Amesville Animal Shelter."

"I like that too," said Florence.

"OK," I said, high-fiving her. "Let's make the best chocolate booth ever!"

"Faster," I said, "or the chocolate will start to harden."

"But it's not right," Florence said, holding her piping bag. She was fussing over the shape of a chocolate heart. It was her third try.

"It doesn't have to be perfect," I said, looking at Florence. "Remember, we have a lot to do." It was Friday night. The Valentine's Day Craft and Bake Sale was the next morning.

"A heart that's not perfect looks more homemade," I said. "That's the point. We don't need perfect. Just good enough."

"*Good enough,*" repeated Florence, softly. "You sound like Miss Delphine."

"Because she's right," I said.

Florence nodded and went faster. As she poured the chocolate, a drop fell onto her hand. When she noticed, she licked it off. She didn't reach for one of her wet cloths. I smiled.

Florence was making progress in more ways than just her writing.

While the hearts were still soft, Florence and I sprinkled candy on them, added the sticks, and then put the tray in the fridge. After they cooled, we took them out and wrote a single letter on each one. We made extras of the letters *L, O, V,* and *E* so people could spell "LOVE" with their lollipops. Florence took her time to make sure each letter looked pretty and well-shaped. This time, I followed *her* pace*. Going slowly meant I was sure to make the letters beautiful.

When we were done, we wrapped the lollipops in cellophane and tied them with bows. All together, they looked like a bouquet of flowers. Mom took pictures and posted them online for our friends and family to see. She showed me her phone. There were lots of likes, thumbs-up, and hearts.

"Stop eating all our chocolate," I scolded Shaya. He'd just eaten a letter *V.*

"It's quality control," he said. "I just want to make sure each chocolate is up to the high standards of the 'Cocoa by Coco' brand."

I grinned. The name for my booth had been Shaya's idea. It made me feel proud.

"I better check an *L* too," he added, "just to be sure." I slapped his hand away as he pretended to reach for an *L*.

"Stop eating and start folding," I told him.

"Yes, boss." He started folding a truffle box. Mom had found them online.

Mika and Roman were supposed to be folding boxes too, but instead they were showing Florence plastic bugs they'd picked out of their Coco's Scream Box. They call it that because whatever's inside makes me scream.

Roman held up a plastic spider.

"When we put this little guy under Coco's pillow we could hear her scream from all the way down the block."

Florence wasn't scared at all.

"That's a tarantula," she said. "If you put that under *my* pillow, I'd know right away it wasn't real. Tarantulas don't live in New England."

As she spoke, Mika and Roman sat down next to her and listened. It was cute seeing them so interested.

"My favorite spider is the wolf spider," she told them. "It's unique because it doesn't make a web. It chases down its prey. Like a wolf."

"That is so cool," said Mika.

"If I were a spider, I'd be a wolf spider because I'm fast!" Roman said.

"Me too!" said Mika. He started howling like a wolf. Florence and Roman starting howling too.

"I still think it's sad you won't be at the sale," I told Florence. "We'd have so much fun."

Shaya, Mika, and Roman all started chanting.

"Come. Come. Come."

Florence shrugged, "Sorry, but I planned the Insectarium visit a long time ago."

"So, we'll put insects in the chocolate," I said. "Just for you."

"Chocolate worms," Roman chimed in, using his spooky voice. "They're delicious."

Before Florence could reply, a car horn honked. I peeked outside the kitchen window. It was Florence's dad. He'd come to take her home. When I looked at the time, I realized it was almost seven. We'd been working for hours.

"Bye, Florence!" I waved to her, as she headed out the door. "Have fun at the Insectarium!"

I watched from the window as Florence climbed into the car. She looked a little distressed. She must have been sad about not joining us for the sale.

I still hoped that, somehow, some way, she'd change her mind.

Chapter Ten

WHAT JUST HAPPENED?

The school gym had turned into a giant buzzing marketplace. Kids, teachers, and parents were setting up their booths. Though the Valentine's Day Craft and Bake Sale wouldn't be open for another hour, people were already lined up outside.

Looking around the gym, it was easy to see why. There was lots of cool stuff to buy. There was a knitting booth, with mittens, hats, and multicolored pom-poms. Beside them, two boys were setting up The Giant Cookie booth. One cookie was the size of my head!

A fourth-grade girl was selling bars of homemade soaps with her mother. Their booth smelled like lavender.

The French teacher, Madame Collette,

had made a bunch of pies, except she didn't call them pies, she called them *tartes*. They looked yummy.

The bead booth was back too. This year the two girls had made pendant necklaces with recycled buttons. I hoped to get one for my mom. We always trade gifts on Valentine's Day.

Mei and Cambi's calligraphy booth was right next to ours. They called it "Write On!" Their cards were hung on a string with tiny, colored clothespins. They also had T-shirts. They'd written messages on them, like "Be Brave," "Girl Power," and "Best Friends Forever."

I thought about what that means. Best Friends Forever.

Mei used to my Best Friend Forever. But I guess the forever part wasn't true anymore. Were we even friends still?

"Your booth is the best. Beautiful menu too," Aunt Joonie said, pointing to a framed chalkboard where I had written down all our products and prices.

Chocolate Heart Lollipops $3 each
Chocolate Letters $2 each
Boxes of LOVE $3 each
Hot Cocoa $2 (includes free vintage teacup!)

I was going to make the menu using our home computer, then print it out. But Miss Delphine told me to take every chance I could to practice my handwriting. I took my time and worked really hard to make the letters look as pretty as the ones in *La Chocolaterie*.

"This is for you," said Aunt Joonie, as she lugged out the old cash register from a box. "You can use it to ring up* all your sales."

The color matched our booth perfectly. Mom laid out tablecloths on the folding tables and strung up our banner of colored fabric. After everything was set up, we looked like a professional *chocolaterie*!

Aunt Joonie was unpacking mismatched

teacups. She had brought a whole bunch from her store. They were for our homemade hot chocolate. I had prepared it this morning. Dad and I had filled three big thermoses full.

As soon as the doors opened, people rushed inside. The gym filled up fast. But something was wrong.

I looked over at Cambi and Mei's booth. A girl was buying a postcard. Next to them, a man with silver hair was buying soap. At Madame Collette's booth, the gym teacher was sampling a forkful of blueberry tarte.

But where were our customers?

That's when I noticed a woman, wearing a green coat, slowly walking by. She was holding hands with a little girl I recognized from the first grade. Seeing our sign, the woman smiled and made her way over. Suddenly, the little girl tugged on her sleeve. The woman stopped and leaned down. The little girl whispered something in ear. The woman looked worried. They turned around and walked quickly in the

opposite direction.

What just happened? What did the girl say to her mother?

A second later, Mika and Roman showed up at our booth. The boys all had early-morning hockey practice, so Dad brought them to the sale afterwards.

"Hey, we heard you guys put worms in the chocolate? Is that true? I mean, when did you do that? We didn't even know!"

I was shocked. "Where did you hear that?"

"The whole school is talking about it," said Roman.

"Who would spread such a rumor*?" Mom wondered.

I looked over at Cambi. She was selling a postcard to the woman with the green coat. As if sensing I was looking her way, she turned and smiled at me.

Could she have done it? Not only did she steal my friend and my job, now she wanted to ruin my chocolate booth?

"Do you really think Cambi would be that mean?" Aunt Joonie asked when I told everyone what I thought. "She knows Mei, and Mei is your friend…"

"But who else would tell everyone we put worms in the chocolate?"

"It was me," I heard a voice say.

I looked up. Florence was standing in front of the chocolate heart lollipops.

"Florence? Aren't you supposed to be at the Insectarium?"

"My father moved our tickets to tomorrow," she explained. "We whited-out the reminder on my calendar, very carefully, so I wouldn't see it, then we put in the new date. I wanted to be here, especially since you told me you'd put worms in the chocolate just for me. I told my friend Frida last night all about it. She said it was a very bad idea and that she should warn people."

"You told her that we had worms in our

chocolate?" I was shocked.

"Yes."

"Why on earth would you say something like that?" my mother asked.

Florence looked at me.

"Coco told me."

"Me?" Then I remembered.

"I *did* say that. To show how much we wanted you to come today. But it was a joke. I totally forgot the Golden Rule of Florence. I should have winked or said ha ha afterwards."

"So, there are no worms in the chocolate?" Florence looked at me.

I shook my head sadly.

That's when Shaya came up to us. He was eating a giant cookie from The Giant Cookie booth.

"Hey, show me the chocolate worms," he said with his mouth full. I sighed.

Our chocolate booth was a total flop.

Chapter Eleven

DO YOU WANT WORMS WITH THAT?

"It's my fault," I said, shaking my head. "I shouldn't have made that joke. Now I've ruined everything. No one will ever buy chocolate from us now. They'll think it's full of worms."

I was mad at myself. *Why was I always blurting things out without thinking?* First with Mei, and now with Florence and my silly bug joke.

"Will this help?" Aunt Joonie asked. She picked up a piece of chalk and wrote on the bottom of the sandwich board:

100% WORM-FREE

Mom and I laughed. Then I got an idea. "Wait—" I said, taking the chalk from her. "I have a better idea." I erased Aunt Joonie's message and wrote:

TRY OUR WORMS!

Florence squinted. "I'm confused. So, we *DO* have chocolate worms?"

"Not yet," I said.

I turned to Shaya. "Can you go to the corner store and get some rainbow jelly worms for me? Get a whole bunch. And go fast!"

Shaya nodded and put on his jacket.

"Use the exit doors by the equipment closet," I instructed him. "They lead straight to the bike racks. It's a shortcut I use when I'm on messenger duty."

Shaya ran for the exit doors as fast as he could.

"OK," I said, rolling up my sleeves. "Now let's get busy."

I quickly unwrapped some chocolate heart lollipops and started breaking them into little pieces.

"You're ruining the hearts!" Mom gasped.

"Trust me," I replied.

I grabbed a few teacups and filled them with the broken chocolate hearts.

When Shaya came back with the worms, I placed a gummy worm on top of each cup.

"See?" I announced, holding up a cup. "It's a Chocolate Worm Feeder!"

"Genius!" said Mom.

"Cool!" said Florence.

"Tasty," said Mika, already helping himself to a worm cup.

That's when the mother with the green coat walked by a second time. She noticed the sign, smiled, and leaned down to speak to her little girl.

"See sweetie, it's a candy worm," I heard her say. "Not a real worm."

The girl nodded and they strolled over. They bought a worm feeder right away, three heart lollipops, and a chocolate letter box. It

was our first big sale of the day.

While they paid for their chocolates, other people came over. And others. And still more. Even Miss Delphine came by.

"Nice sign," she said, looking at our chalkboard.

"Thanks," I replied.

"You've come a long way, girls. I'm so proud of you."

"We'll see at the next spelling test," I said. "I hope Miss Pennyfield can read my writing." So far, I hadn't been able to get the hang of writing well on tests. Miss Delphine said it was normal in stressful situations and that I'd get used to it.

"I'm sure you'll do great," she said. "Now, please give me one of those worm feeders. My nephew is going to love it." She handed me a five-dollar bill.

When I opened the cash register it was overflowing with coins and bills.

"The I CAN room is going to get a lot of

money for new supplies," Florence said.

"I'll put it to good use," Miss Delphine promised.

After that, I can barely remember taking a break. We were so busy. Cocoa by Coco was a sweet success!

⚜

"There's hardly anything left," I said, putting the last chocolate heart lollipop in a bag and handing it to a customer.

Other booths were packing up too. Cocoa by Coco and The Giant Cookie booth were the last ones standing.

"I'm so glad I came," said Florence. "I wouldn't have wanted to miss out on this for anything, not even for a luna moth."

"Or a red-fanged funnel spider?" I said.

"Not even."

Since getting to know Florence, I had learned a lot about bugs. And I wanted to know more. So, we both decided we should go to the Insectarium *together*.

As I erased our menu board, I felt my stomach rumble.

"I'm hungry," I said. We'd all been so busy selling chocolates, there had been no time for a snack.

"I have a banana and two apples in my purse," said Mom.

"I have a bag of pretzels," said Aunt Joonie, pulling out a bag from her purse.

I looked around the booth. There were still a few of our chocolate letters.

"We could melt the leftover letters and do a fondue!" I suggested. "After selling chocolate all day, I think we deserve a little chocolate just for us."

Everyone agreed this was a good idea.

I took the fastest route I knew to the I CAN room, where the microwave was. Florence came with me, and luckily Miss Delphine was there to help. In a few moments, I had a bowlful of melted chocolate, ready to go.

Florence opened the door for me and very carefully, very slowly, I carried the bowl of melted chocolate out into the hallway. I'd learned from Miss Delphine how going fast wasn't always a good idea. If Florence's lesson was "good enough," mine was "it's not a race."

That's when it happened. A thud. A shriek. A splash. The sticky, disastrous mess that brings me back to the beginning of my story.

There I was, suddenly holding an empty bowl. In front of me, mouth open in shock, was Cambi Laflamme, completely covered in chocolate fondue.

Chapter Twelve

THE FLYING FONDUE RETURNS

Cambi was frozen speechless. Chocolate dripped off her sweater onto the floor. Other students from the sale gathered around to watch.

"I don't know how it happened!" I told Mrs. Hayward.

"Oh really?" Mrs. Hayward glared at me with her laser beam eyes.

"Are you sure you weren't speeding again, Cordelia?" she said.

She reached for her pocket. *Does she keep speeding tickets in the pocket of her weekend jogging suit?* I wondered. *Would I finally know what terrible things happen when you get three speeding tickets?*

I was ready to find out, when suddenly I remembered what Miss Delphine had asked me when we first started making chocolate letters: *Do you prefer your chocolate in your tummy or on the floor?*

I knew the answer. *In my tummy*. And certainly *not* on anybody's sweater.

"Wait!" I said, at the top of my voice. "I wasn't speeding. I was taking my time. I was being careful. I knew I was carrying a bowl of melted chocolate and I was going slowly. I was paying attention." As I said the words out loud, I realized these were all the things I'd learned in the I CAN room.

Mrs. Hayward looked doubtful. How could I make her believe me?

"Actually, I'm the one who was running," Cambi suddenly confessed. We all looked at her in surprise. The chocolate statue had, at last, spoken.

"I was in the car with my parents, ready to head home, when I remembered that I didn't buy my grandmother a Valentine's Day gift. I wanted to get her a chocolate heart before you closed."

I saw Cambi was holding a twenty-dollar bill. It had chocolate on it too.

"I was running very fast and not looking where I was going," Cambi continued. "*I* ran into Coco. It wasn't the other way around."

"Oh," said Mrs. Hayward. "Thank you for being so honest, Cambi."

I was grateful too. I wondered if I was wrong about her. Maybe Cambi wasn't a friend-stealing, job-stealing, booth-ruining villain*. Maybe it was just me, feeling I wasn't good enough. But now that I was more confident about everything, including my handwriting, I felt different about Cambi too.

"Would you like a homemade wet wipe?" Florence asked Cambi. She rifled through her backpack and pulled out a wet cloth. "I always carry some around, in case I get something sticky on me."

"Thanks Florence," Cambi said, taking the cloth. "But I think I might need the whole pack."

"Sorry about your butterfly sweater," I said. I doubted it would ever come clean.

"It's all right," she said, "At least now I get to try some of your chocolate." She lifted her finger and peeled some chocolate from the butterfly's face. She tasted it.

"Very good."

Everybody laughed, even Mrs. Hayward.

ॐ ॐ

"Please open up your notebooks and get your pencils ready." Miss Pennyfield was standing at the chalkboard, holding her list of spelling words.

I took a breath.

I'd memorized all our new vocabulary words the night before. I knew all the words by heart. But could I write them well enough for

Miss Pennyfield to read them?

I opened my notebook, then looked across the room at Cambi and Mei. They gave me a thumbs-up sign. It was their way of saying "good luck."

Since the Valentine's Day Craft and Bake Sale, a lot had changed. I was finally invited to join the Calligraphy Club. Cambi wanted to learn how to make chocolate letters. Florence was invited too. Ever since Cambi realized butterflies were a type of insect, she and Florence had a lot to talk about.

I gave them the thumbs-up sign back. Then I heard a voice speak up from beside me.

"You ready, Coco?"

Florence was seated at the desk next to mine. She had moved from Mrs. Huntsberger's class into my class. Thanks to all her hard work in the I CAN room, Miss Delphine said she was ready for a new challenge. And I had a new friend. (Scaly and Slimy seemed to like her too.)

"I'm ready, Florence."

I took a deep breath, picked up my pencil, and imagined it was chocolate.

Glossary

Many words have more than one meaning. Here are the definitions of words marked with this symbol * (an asterisk) as they are used in sentences.

autism: *a developmental disorder that appears in children, who may have trouble with social and communication skills, repeat certain actions over and over, or become upset with changes in routine. It can affect the way someone learns, thinks, and solves problems*

baking sheets: *flat metal trays often used for baking cookies*

bitter: *having a sharp taste; not sweet*

boutique: *a small shop that sells specialty items that are well-crafted and carefully chosen*

calligraphy: *decorative handwriting or lettering*

capital: *an uppercase letter used for proper names or places and at the beginning of a sentence*

fine motor skills: *using small muscles, like those in your wrists, hands, and fingers, in coordination with your eyes for such things as writing, grasping small objects, and fastening clothing*

heads: *in handwriting, the top part of a letter (such as b, d, k) that is above the baseline of that letter*

"high time": *it is now time to do something that should have been done a long time ago*

"in a daze": *confused and unable to act in a normal way*

literally: *in an exact way*

lit up: *suddenly looked excited*

loco: *crazy; in Britain, it can also mean a high-speed train locomotive—both describe Coco!*

occupational therapist: *in a school, a specially trained person who helps children learn through play how to manage difficulties they have doing certain activities*

pace: *the speed at which something is done*

parchment paper: *a type of paper, often used in baking to prevent items from sticking to the pan*

piping bag: *a cone-shaped bag fitted with a metal tip that can be filled with frosting and used for decorating or writing on cakes*

rhinestones: *sparkly glass stones meant to look like diamonds or other gems*

rifled: *searched through something in a hurried way*

ring up: *use the numbered keys on a cash register to record and add up your sales*

ruby: *the red color of a gemstone*

rumor: *a story that is going around that may or may not be true*

scrumptious: *delicious*

sequences: *the particular order or steps in which something should be done*

stampeded: *ran in a wild rush*

tails: *in handwriting, the bottom part of a letter (such as j, p,) that is below the baseline of that letter*

technique: *a way of doing something using a special skill*
truffles: *small candy balls made of chocolate*
villain: *the "baddie" in a story*

this is our story

We are an extraordinary generation of children. And have we got a story to tell.

Our Generation® is unlike any that has come before. We're making a positive impact on our community by performing small, but powerful, acts of kindness, standing tall for causes we believe in, and creating a narrative where everyone can make a difference.

We're speaking up for those around us, taking leaps to develop big ideas, and embracing new opportunities without ever forgetting to build lasting memories along the way. From playing sports outdoors and learning new instruments, to singing out loud and dancing around, we're laughing together with friends as we share in the best moments of being a kid.

Our dreams have no limits, our voices echo around every corner, and we have the strongest belief that we can make anything and everything possible with our greatest gift: imagination.

This is our time. This is our story.

ourgeneration.com

About the Author

*Laura Leigh Motte is an author,
screenwriter, mother, and lover of
chocolate. This is her fifth
Our Generation® book.*

About the Illustrator

*Passionate about drawing from an early age, Géraldine Charette
decided to pursue her studies in computer multimedia in order to further
develop her style and technique. Her favorite themes to explore in her
illustrations are fashion and urban life. In her free time, Géraldine loves
to paint and travel. She is passionate about horses and loves spending
time at the stable. It's where she feels most at peace and gives her time to
think and fuel her creativity.*

*Writing with Chocolate became the book that you are holding in your
hands with the assistance of the talented people at Maison Battat Inc.,
including Joe Battat, Dany Battat, Loredana Ramacieri, Sandy Jacinto,
Véronique Casavant, Cynthia Lopez, Laurie Gaudreau-Levesque,
Alexandra Bonfà, Ananda Guarany, Jenny Gambino, Arlee Stewart,
Natalie Cohen, Sophie Trudel, Zeynep Yasar, Joanne Burke Casey, and
Pamela Shrimpton.*

*A special thanks from the author to Valentina Quan, developmental
editor, and to Delphine Vincent and Ashley Carruth, the occupational
therapists who consulted on this story.*